New Chip and Other Stories
Femdom Mind Control
Flash Fiction – Vol. 20

S.B.

Table of Contents

It's time to change the way you think.

A shoutout to all patrons of Spell… B-O-U-N-D

for the ongoing support.

Addicted

Dating Theresa hadn't really been my choice, but an imposition from the highest spheres of power. The young nurse was the only daughter of a respectable Senator we were extremely interested in controlling to extend our influence in American politics but, to do that, it was best to have her at our mercy first. Being one of the finest hypnotists in the Group, I got the job and a lot more than I bargained for. She had an incredible resilience to any attempt to mess with her mind and an even greater cunning when it came to juggling with mine...

One day, I stopped by her house at her request. I wasn't feeling too well, courtesy of a full week of sleepless nights. She took me to the master bedroom and asked me to sit on the bed. I did without so much of a thought, not even blinking when she said she had some questions for me and that I had to answer them truthfully.

"Okay." I nodded.

"First question." Theresa cupped my chin. "Why did you really come to talk to me in the hospital a month ago?"

"I was told to by the organization I'm part of. My orders were to seduce and turn you into our hypno-puppet to gain leverage over your mother." I responded, surprised for spewing my guts just like that.

"I suspected as much. It seems the intel I got beforehand was accurate after all. Now, why do you think you revealed those things to me so easily?"

"I..." my head tilted awkwardly, a premonition of a future bow. "I don't know. I feel so..."

"Weak?"

"Yes."

"Good. That's how you're supposed to feel."

It was only then I took notice of the bottle of pills she was holding, the vitamin supplement that had been a part of my routine even before I met her. "No, you didn't..."

"Of course, I did, silly. You've been such a good boy willingly drugging yourself for me. It takes a while for the hypnotic compound to take hold of your neural pathways, but your behavior in the last couple of days makes it clear you're ready for the taking. My bosses will be pleased."

"Who... who do you work for?"

"I ask the questions here and it's not for you to know. The only thing that matters is that your little shadow government won't be around for much longer once your body and mind finally betray you. You're already addicted. Soon, you'll have no choice but to obey me."

I looked at her in awe, fully aware that I had been outplayed and yet equally conscious of the contradictory needs growing inside. She was right. Despite her disturbing revelations, my trembling soul was already aching for those pink pills...

Banquet

The alien entity first came into contact with The Excelsior after a forced stop for repairs near Quadrant Alpha Zed 22. It was the farthest a Class L spaceship had ever traveled since the discovery of stable wormholes, a promise of exploration no one could thwart. Or so they thought.

First sighting occurred less than five minutes upon arrival to the area and first contact another five minutes after that. The images originally recorded by the bio-organic cameras running along Corridor B8's primary structures were vague, but the ship's AI could extrapolate its true nature, nonetheless. Silicon-based signature, faint traces of radioactivity, optical mimicry capabilities. It roamed across the lower decks, tricking unsuspecting crew members with its illusions. Less than two thousand seconds later, there was no one alive to tell the tale anymore.

One by one, everyone else suffered the same fate, their bodies suddenly stopping in their tracks as if they had lost all will to live. The Captain was one of the last to go, eyes flooded with blinding light. Only the chief pilot remained locked to his console in a living nightmare. He was still there when the entity came to meet him under the guise of everyone he held dear.

He saw his college crush, his three-months pregnant wife, his baby sister, his mother and all the other women he would happily do anything for. He was still seeing them when effulgent tendrils broke the spell and wrapped around his neck. When they finally receded, he rose from the bloody seat, vitreous eyes devoid of any rational thought. Reality was clearer now, and he knew exactly what to do.

Taking the ship's controls, he set a course to Earth, grinning sheepishly from ear to ear. Mistress deserved another banquet.

Boob Drone

Charles peeked through the keyhole of his sister's bedroom and squinted. Was that a naked Mr. Rogers on her bed, eyes glazed like he was high or something? What the fuck? Brenda had always been an outgoing woman, even more so now that she had turned eighteen, but that didn't explain what she was doing with their old Math teacher. Was she really that desperate for a fuck that even a late sexagenarian would do?

"Not on my watch." He rotated the door handle, only to find it locked. "Okay," He thought, cell in hand. "Time to warn Mom and Dad of what's going on in their house. I'm sure they'll be thrilled."

Before he could make the call, the young brunette appeared from behind him and snatched the phone, giggling. "What do you think you're doing, big brother?"

"N-nothing." He stammered as he turned to look her way. Despite being three years older, Charles had always been intimidated by her ever since they were kids. There was something about her peering gaze that made his knees tremble like jelly, but that wasn't the worst. No, she had a powerful weapon by her side whenever she wanted something out of him. Two, in fact. She had boobs.

The big, round juicy breasts were almost completely exposed under the low-cut pink top, jiggling beauties of mesmeric intent that made his mouth water. It was wrong to have such dirty thoughts about his baby sister, yet it was also almost impossible to resist.

"You were never a good liar, Charlie." She swayed her bosom. "Mom and Dad need not know what is happening here."

"And what exactly is happening?"

"Oh, I think you know. I'm having fun, of course. Mr. Rogers is one of my favorite boob drones. I love seeing him go under and be completely powerless to resist me, don't you?"

"No! You're sick, Brenda! Wake him up right now!"

"No can do, I'm afraid. The drone hasn't served his purpose today, yet. And frankly, neither have you, but that can be... rectified."

Brenda cupped her breasts and gave them a firm squeeze, erect nipples overwhelming his senses. Charles stumbled backwards as if he had been hit by a powerful uppercut, memories of past conditioning resurfacing inside his mind.

"That's right, sweetie, you're a boob drone, too. That's all you'll ever be when I wish to be entertained, and this is your chance to do it. Sink deeper for me now and remember your place. You will obey my boobs."

"Yes, Brenda." He sheepishly droned just like she had programmed him to do. Once a boob drone, always a boob drone, no memories required unless that was her will.

"Such a good boy. It's so much when you don't have to think for yourself, isn't it? Now, follow me inside and let's see how two horny pets get along together...."

Dear Brother

BREAKING NEWS: NEW AMAZONIAN MOVEMENT WINS THE ELECTION. FIRST FEMALE-LED GOVERNMENT IN OVER ONE HUNDRED AND FIFTY YEARS.

"Dear brother,

What you've always said it would happen, eventually did. I never believed it would be possible and yet, here we are. The NAM is government, and the truth is nobody knows what to expect, myself included. I confess I'm a bit scared. I wish you were still around so we could talk about this. Retirement isn't fun without you."

IS THE NEW GOVERNMENT LED BY DANIELLE FARIS GOING TO CHANGE THE EDUCATION SYSTEM? MORE AT 11.

"Dear brother,

They have announced the new government program. One of the key proposals is a reinforcement of all sectors of our educational system. Rumor has it they're planning on calling back old teachers into action. Can't say I'm thrilled at the idea, but I'm not really used to having so much free time on my hands so... we'll see what happens. I miss you."

BREAKING NEWS: EDUCATIONAL REFORM UNDER WAY AFTER "G-BILL" IS APPROVED BY A MAJORITY OF TWO-THIRDS.

"Dear brother,

I got a letter from the Ministry of Education officially informing me I'm being reinstated effective immediately with double pay to assist on the transition to the new system. This is so weird, and it's happening so fast. Remember when we had to wait two months just for a debate at the Parliament and then at least two more months before they approved any structural bill? The NEM did it in less than three weeks! I'm impressed. I never thought they had it in them. Still a bit suspicious of this so-called reform, but I'll take the pay, anyway. How hard can this be?"

NEVER HAS A GOVERNMENT APPOINTED MORE WOMEN FOR KEY SECTORS IN EDUCATION. MEET

ALL THE NEW FACES AND WHAT WE CAN EXPECT FROM THEM LATER AT 10.

"Dear brother,

Today was my first day back at Wilmington College. It's still the same architectural mess we love, but can you believe it's all been painted in light pink? They gave me our old office back, but it seems I'll be sharing it with Hope Lewis this time around. You remember Hope, don't you? She used to have this major crush on you back in the day. I can tell you her sense of humor is still intact. I think I'll enjoy working alongside her in this new adventure."

BREAKING NEWS: NAM GOVERNMENT UNVEILS NEW TEACHER'S WEBSITE.

"Dear brother,

First, forgive me for not visiting you last month, but things have been a little hectic at College. New directives keep arriving that change the way we're used to lecture. First were the new manuals which contain some of the strangest revisionist History I've ever seen and now it's this website: nev-edu.com. I just exited a ten-hour training program to learn to use this tool, and it's kind of preposterous. They want us to log in every day before the first class and after the last one, without exception. They say it's for 'mere statistical purposes' but it still feels like some sort of control mechanism unbefitting of a Democracy, especially when it seems female teachers are exempt from it. Hope says my concerns are frivolous, but I've written a letter to the Ministry of Education today expressing my disdain for this extra measure. I'll let you know what their response is the moment I get it.

WHAT ARE 'EDUCATIONAL BRACELETS' AND WHAT IS THEIR PURPOSE IN THE NEW EDUCATIONAL SYSTEM? FIND OUT MORE THIS WEEKEND.

"Dear brother,

It's been five weeks since I sent that letter and my concerns remain unaddressed. Things are getting every stranger now. I continue to have to log in at the website every day, but now I have to do it whenever I go out to lunch or need to go to the bathroom, too. There's no way this has any statistical intent, but I'm not allowed to complain. I tried skirting my responsibilities once and immediately got a 5% pay reduction. The website's garish colors give me headaches and I'm pretty sure they're affecting my sleep too, but what can I do? To make matters worse, all male teachers have to wear these new leather bracelets now. They're our new rating system. We're constantly being tested by our female peers and students to see if we're upholding the rules. It makes no sense! I'm terrified, brother! How did it come to this and what's going to happen next?"

BREAKING NEWS: MINISTRY OF EDUCATION TO BE RENAMED MINISTRY OF GYNARCHIC SPLENDOR.

"Dear brother,

I can't stay for long. I have to go back to College in ten. After four months of this, I think it's safe to say I'm no longer a teacher but something else. I'm monitored at all times, my thoughts are irrelevant. These bracelets are nothing more than legalized shock collars that women can trigger at will. Hope loves to activate mine and so do my 'students'. Yesterday, I spent the whole first period kneeling on the floor while they humiliated me and the other men around. I think something more happened, but I... I can't remember. I think it's the website. It's doing something to my... my... huh, what was I saying? I have to go back. I'm sorry, brother, I have to go back before they punish me."

SIX MONTHS INTO NAM'S GOVERNMENT. IS THIS THE END OF THE MALE GENDER AS WE KNOW IT OR IS IT NATURAL EVOLUTION? FIND OUT AT 11.

"Dear brother,

This is the last time I'm coming here to talk to you. I don't have permission, and that's okay. All male servants must obey their female superiors, no exceptions. Wilmington College is being reconverted into a Gynarchic Programming Center, the first of many. I'm happy to be at the vanguard of such an important achievement. My new role is to guide all hapless young men into accepting their role in this new world, always properly supervised, of course. I can't be trusted with freedom. I'm so happy I won't have to bother with it ever again. It's such a joyous day! Too bad you're not here to see it. I will always love you, but I adore Women even more. They are Goddesses and I must serve them. It is my honor to comply. Goodbye."

Gateway to Paradise

Alyssa scrambled to get the house keys and finally entered her house. It was half-past seven on a Friday afternoon and the weather was atrocious, courtesy of a tropical cyclone that didn't know when to go away. She was tired. Work at the office was getting increasingly more demanding as the Holiday Season drew near, and she was out of vacation days for the rest of the year. The last four weeks promised to be Hell on Earth but, fortunately for her, she had a personal gateway to Paradise at the click of a button.

The nearing thirties secretary closed the front door behind her, took off her wet parka and muddy shoes, and proceeded to her bedroom on the upper level where a reflective black mp3 player laid between the pillows of her queen-size bed, waiting to be put to good use again. It had been a birthday present from Her Goddess, the impossibly entrancing woman who had shown her her true purpose in life. Ever since she had found her online one year prior, she had never looked back, finally embracing her future every single day.

Alyssa opened the cupboard next to the bed and laid down a square blanket on the floor. It was her worshiping spot, the designated place for her communion with Goddess. Air pods on her ears, the busty redhead closed her eyes and smiled.

Goddess' tender voice immediately resonated inside her soul, triggering the perfect response she loved so much. She was the most beautiful person in the world, her wishes could not be denied. And what Goddess wanted more than everything was for her to shed her artificial persona, the false name her parents gave her at birth, and repeat the designation that bound her to true bliss.

Drone A29, mindless cog in her perpetual hive mind, an object that lived to expose herself on camera for Her pleasure and the pleasure of those She shared Her toy with. A half an hour reminder session before dinner was exactly she needed to feel whole again before the next pleasurable humiliation. Alyssa's eyes fluttered as she abandoned her human voice and embraced the monotone rhythm of brainwashing, running through her lips like sweet liqueur. Goddess was all. That was the way the world worked.

It's good to be a drone. Drone will always obey.

Inevitable

"There is nothing you can do to stop me. Absolutely nothing. My house, my rules. Breaking you was always part of the plan, and I always stick to my plans. You should know that by now. You were destined to be mine and love to follow my lead no matter what happened.

"Do not give me that look. It was inevitable. From the moment we met, and you could not stop staring into my gorgeous emerald eyes, I knew this is how things would play out. Sure, it may have taken longer for you to realize it, but that is because you are a male and will always be three steps behind me. Your resistance and overt defiance to my wishes was predicted, analyzed, and swiftly counteracted, and now here we are, my superior will becoming all you can think of, my thoughts completely overriding yours. This is right. It will be nothing else but that.

"Keep looking at me, completely focused on my words. Each one causes a tingle in your body, a feeling of rippling euphoria so intense you just cannot help but drool. Do it for me. Do not stop salivating your life away. It entertains me to see you helplessly lose control of yourself, reduced to primary instincts and an overwhelming need to surrender. You are a pet. You have always been a pet. You will be nothing other than a pet. Pets can and will be trained. Pets can and will be obedient. You will always obey my commands on your fours, eyes lowered to the floor, tail wagging between your legs. You cannot fight. You will never fight me again.

"In a moment, I am going to snap my fingers. This will be your cue to completely embrace what I expect of you from now on. You will never eat from the table again. The bowl before you is your future. When you hear the snap, you will stick your tongue in it and start munching. The more you do, the less you will think about human food. You do not deserve it. You are just a pet. Obey your owner, pet. You have no choice."

snap

Trevor opened the kitchen door and peeked inside just in time to see his girlfriend Abby being licked in the face by an overly energetic one year and a half brown and white Shih Tzu. Phone in hand, he started recording the scene for posterity.

"Were you just trying to hypnotize the dog again right now?" He cracked a mischievous smile. "You'll never be able to do that, you know?"

"Yeah..." Abby turned his way, golden locks of hair cascading over her pearly lips. "I keep forgetting he's not as easy as you."

snap

As the small dog continued to revel in its incessant urge to kiss her favorite human, Trevor laid the phone on the

marble counter and rushed to the blue plastic bowl, happy
to please her too once again.

Merry Christmas?

"Ho, ho, and ho... step right in!" Santa said to the three leather-clad prostitutes as he opened the left rear door of his rental car.

"Oh..." One of them, a curvy brunette in seven-inch heels, said. "Have we been naughty this year?"

"You're always naughty and you know it, but I'm happy to reward you for that." Santa replied, waving a stack of Benjamin Franklin's on his left hand.

"Just my kind of present..." The second hooker's blue eyes gleamed with joy.

"Santa" was actually Dave Reuben, and Dave was a lawyer. A good one, despite lacking moral fiber and always choosing the wrong side of History. The fat outfit and white beard were the not so proud leftovers of a company's Christmas party from years back which he had never returned and were as good enough of a disguise to avoid indiscreet traffic cameras in his pursuit of illicit sex. Already a regular in all the shady circuits in town, the dirty Mr. Claus loved when pussies outnumbered erect cocks and three had always been a favorite.

The shady motel room that followed was alive with copious sounds of senseless fornication when the three women became four and Dave blinked to make sure he was not seeing things. The newcomer - a radiant blonde that didn't look a day older than twenty-five - sat at the edge of the bed, wearing a red and black trumpet dress and enough attitude to melt The North Pole.

"What are you doing here?" She asked, disdainfully and, as she spoke, Time all around stopped except for the two of them. "Didn't I lock you up in the toy factory earlier today?"

"Hmmm..." Dave surveyed the room, befuddled at seeing his exotic company suddenly reduced to life-size statues in the most awkward positions imaginable. "Who are you and what the fuck just happened?"

"Don't play games with me, Ni... oh!" The mysterious lady dropped the sentence midway. "You're not him! Fuck!"

"Him who?" The lawyer muttered, still trying to process the impossibility of what he was seeing.

"Nick, Nicholas, Santa... you know. My husband is quite the cheating douchebag, but everyone loves him because of all the gifts and shit. I don't get it!"

"Santa? So, you're telling me you're Mrs. Claus? Cute! Who are you really, and who put you up to this?"

"I am who I just said I am, and it seems my jealousy is to blame." She smirked. "I'm always to trying to find evidence of his wrongdoings and when I saw you and your partners hitting along, I assumed the worst. Friendly advice: ditch the red, it doesn't look good on you at all. Bye!"

"Wait!"

"What is it?"

"You can't just leave them frozen! Not when we were having so much fun."

"Oh, right! Sorry. Carry on, then."

Time resumed its normal flow as she vanished in thin air right before his incredulous gaze. "Merry... Christmas?" He muttered as the iniquitous trio continued their feast of depravity.

Less than a minute later, she was back again, brooding eyes eager for something else. The hookers froze once more, two of them right in the middle of a long, wet kiss.

"On second thought, you're just like him, aren't you?" She said. "I bet you have a wife and kids at home and here you are, frolicking around with others without a care in the world. I won't have that. Not on my watch."

Mrs. Claus snapped her fingers, a knife appearing in her right hand. No one should celebrate Christmas without a tree and no tree should be devoid of balls...

New Chip

"Ah, look who rejoined us in the world of the living. You had us worried there for a second. Can you move? No, don't bother trying to say anything for now, just follow this light with your eyes. Left and right. Left and right. Good.

I can see you're confused, so let me clear things for you because I know it will make you feel better. My name is Dr. Bethany Carmichael and you're at my clinic. I've been a friend of your owner since college days. She brought you here after your chip malfunctioned and shut down your brain. We had to induce a light coma to perform a replacement surgery but now you're upgraded with all the bells and whistles a mindfucked slave to perform accordingly. I'm going to let you rest for a bit, get your normal functions to resume, and then I'll return to verify your new skills, okay? Close your eyes again and sleep, dreaming of her and how lucky you are to be controlled. Good boy."

(...)

"Wake up, slave! Your latest test results are in and it seems you've recovered up to 99% of your previous brain capacity, more than enough for what's expected of you.

Now, your owner is busy enslaving another pet, so she gave me carte blanche in the meantime. I've adjusted the chip's frequency so that your mind automatically responds to my voice and my commands. My royal title has also been imprinted in its core programming, so you should already know the proper way to address me from now on. What is my royal name?"

"Queen Bethany."

"Correct. Queen of your thoughts, ruler of all (for the time being, at least). Refusing me is not an option. You will please your owner by making sure I'm pleased as well. You should have all your motor skills by now, so I'm ordering you to get out of bed and kneel before me.

Very good, slave. The numbers don't lie. Your compliance response was three times faster than ever recorded by your old chip but, in time, you'll be even more efficient, I can assure you. The new subroutines take a while to be properly integrated into your central nervous system but, once they do, the neural pathways are permanent. How does this make you feel?"

"Wonderful, Queen Bethany. Thank you."

"You're welcome, slave. Nothing makes me happier than putting the likes of you in their proper place. It's the primary reason I started this project after all. Now, let me fine-tune these parameters..."

"Hmmm, oh... that..."

"... is wonderful, I'm sure. You've just experienced the bliss of ten orgasms, slave, and I can crank up to one hundred if you're completely obedient as you should be. Of course, the opposite is also true. I have also defined new pain thresholds for when you try to resist your conditioning so here's a little taste at -5."

"Oh.... FUUUUUCK!"

"Hurts like a bitch, doesn't it? And that's one of the lowest intensities. Thank me for not going higher this time."

"Th... ank you, Q-queen Bethany."

"Much better, but here comes the best part. Your owner told me she wasn't pleased with your anal surrender, so let's give it another go. Ass up, slave!

"That's right. Spread it for me. I have this nice big black cock here, waiting for your submission. You will take everything I want, just like you will take everything she wants. Right now, you're just one big orifice attached to a body. Orifices don't think, they're just filled. Goddesses always get what's theirs. Take my cock, slave! Take it like the walking hole you are! Take it and thank me again!"

"Thank you, Queen Bethany."

"Louder."

"Thank... hm... you, Queen Bethany!"

"I said: Louder!"

"THANK YOU, QUEEN BETHANY! THANK YOU, THANK YOU.... oh.... THANK YOU!"

"That's a good bitch. Not bad for a first run, but since your owner is not back for a day or so, you can handle a few more, right? Of course, you can! Take a minute to wipe that stupid drool off your face and then we shall continue."

Reset

Amanda looked down at the pet curled up on the metal table, unable to stop the tears from rolling down her red cheeks. It was the day of her 27th birthday and the saddest one in memory.

"Must we really?" She bawled, petite hands covering her Greek nose.

"Yes." Dr. Walters replied, hypodermic needle on the ready. "And the sooner the better."

"But I don't want to! It's not fair! He's my favorite pet in the whole world!" Amanda leaned against the table, dirty red hair falling over its chin.

"I know but once you reach this degenerative state, it's the most humane thing to do."

"There has to be another way, something else we haven't tried!"

"Honey, there isn't. We've been through this so stop torturing yourself. I've been doing for more than twenty years and the alternative is far less agreeable. You don't want to go through the agony of watching it wither any further. Let me administer the shot. We have a dozen of replacements in the back waiting for a chance if you decide to change your mind afterward."

"How dare you speak of replacements!" The pet owner vociferated. Were she not learning to control her temper, she would have cracked her skull on the spot.

"I'm merely trying to do what's best for you and this is it. I know it will never be the same but it's just the end of a cycle, nothing more."

"Fine!" Amanda retreated to the other end of the room, back against the wall. "Do it already and put me out of my misery."

"You're doing the right thing." The doctor picked up the syringe and blocked the view with her light blue lab coat. It was a quick job, the cool liquid inside the barrel finding it way into the agonizing companion. The pet squirmed on the table, exhaled one last painful breath and then...

... stood up, eyes defocused, its language skills returning but none of its previous memories. He stared blankly at the two women, a single drop of blood marking the spot where the needle had reset its entire existence.

"Welcome back, slave." Dr. Walters said.

"I'm sorry, do I know you?"

"You used to, but you'll do it again in time."

"What happened?"

"Your NAM-approved identification implant reached the end of its lifespan but, instead of safely decomposing inside your body, it started poisoning it, instead. You would have perished in terrible pain in the coming months had we not intervened. Unfortunately, the cure also required a complete synaptic rewrite. Do you understand?"

"I... no, not really."

"Well, that's irrelevant anyway. This is your owner. She will take good care of you going forward."

"Ah, yes... of course." He mumbled, lost in Amanda's spellbinding visage. "Forgive me for not recognizing you. It seems I lost a significant part of me."

"You did, but it's not your fault." The younger woman held his hands together and kissed them. "Stupid technology! Don't worry. I'll train you again to my liking and everything will be all right, I promise."

"Thank you." He instinctively dropped to his knees. "It's what I want the most in this world."

"See?" Dr. Walters lit up a cigarette and smirked. "And you were crying your eyes out just now! Not everyone has the chance to completely start over in a Mistress/slave relationship, so you better make it count."

"I will." Amanda nodded, pressing his head against her thighs. Even without his memories, he was still hers to command. The new training program would start right away.

Stranger than Fiction

The so-called "Leader of the Free World" was on a social media rampage once again, trying to will alternate realities into existence by the sheer power of senseless vitriol. The headlines practically wrote themselves, a terrible situation exacerbated to exhaustion with each unhinged repetition.

"I Won! I Won it all! I always win! Why won't 'they' admit the truth? NOT LEAVING! #sad.

In the last three hours, he had tweeted in all caps fifteen times, posted three self-congratulatory videos on Facebook, shared a video of himself looking at the mirror while singing 'Hail to the Chief', and posed for a Christmas postcard while having his ass kissed by his son-in-law, as millions around the world worshiped his nonsense and millions more cried out in utter despair.

Outside the slightly ovoid office decorated with beautiful desks, beautiful chairs, beautiful lamps, beautiful phones painted in the most beautiful sheen of black and red and, of course, the most beautiful name plaques in the world, three of his assistants were facepalming left and right.

"Is he still going?" The first one asked.

"Yeah. He started early today and doesn't seem like he wants to stop." The second one replied.

"This is getting embarrassing! We must do something! The third one concluded.

"I already tried everything I could think of!"

"Absolutely everything?"

"Yes. The hamburger trail led nowhere, and the edited news clips lost him after a minute."

"How about sneaking up some hookers through the backdoor?"

"Done that too, and no response. All he does is spew gibberish after gibberish and... fuck, he did it again! Look at this shit!"

"170.000 Martian ballots beamed to Earth on Election Night! Illegal aliens! Supreme Court must intervene for the sake of our Democracy!"

"Can we sedate his coffee and have him sleep the next forty days?"

"He's so high already, sedatives don't work on him anymore. Admit it, we're fucked!"

"Not quite. I just remembered something."

"What?"

"I know someone. Let me see if I can get her on the line."

"Hurry. He's taking another sel... Oh my God, is that his daughter between his legs?"

* * *

General Rupert Hayes blinked when he answered Alexandra's phone. He didn't remember when he had been assigned the role of her personal secretary, but that was okay. At least, he wasn't naked this time around.

"Alexandra?"

"Yes, General?"

"You're needed at The White House. Something about a raving lunatic pretending to be a man..."

"I was wondering when they would call me. This is going to be fun. Don't wait for me."

"Yes, Alexandra. Anything you say."

* * *

Two hours later, the secret agent/hypnotist entered the lame duck's refuge. The diapered seventy-year-old had traded orange for gray, but it's not like the new color suited him, anyway.

"Who are you?" He immediately asked.

"I wish I could say I'm the answer to all your problems, but that is a bit too much even for me." Alexandra retorted.

"Well, whatever... I won and you're hot. Come here and let me grab you by the pussy."

"Not going to happen."

"But I'm famous, and when you're famous, people let me do it. Spread them, bitch!"

"You can't do whatever comes to mind. Not with me, at least. However, you can look at this and relax..." She produced a shiny red pin with his favorite slogan inscribed on it.

"Hypnosis? That's for dumb suckers. And I'm smart, like really, really smart. My IQ is off the charts and people tell me I have all the best words, too."

"I just need one for you: sleep!"

And for the first time in almost four years, there was complete and utter silence in the room.

BREAKING NEWS: Outgoing President apologizes to the world for all his faults with a dildo stuck up his ass! Stay tuned.

Sweet Music

"Hi, Mom,

I don't know why I gave you a smartphone when you never answer my calls. Anyway, I hope you've been doing well. Just wanted to let you know the transfer is finally happening. I'm the new priest at St. Wellington's Church, near Wilmington College. It's a great honor for me to be of service at such a prestigious location. Sadly, with everything the transfer entails, I won't be able to travel there for Thanksgiving. I'm sorry, but I hope you understand. I'll call you again when I can. Please pick up the phone next time."

(...)

Excerpts from the journal of Father Theodore Mason

November 27th, 2120,

First day at the new Parish. Still trying to settle in. I was hoping to avoid living in the clergy house, but finding a place for myself has been a nightmare so it will have to do for the time being. It's a nice place around five blocks from the church, and the exercise going back and forth is sure to do me good, at least. Two other priests are staying here with me for now, but we haven't had the chance to get to know each other just yet. Perhaps soon.

November 29th, 2120,

I've held my first service today and was surprised at the massive turnout, a stark contrast to where I used to be before. People sure love the church around here, and that's an excellent thing. There were a lot of couples, young and old, and all had one thing in common. The men were all deferential to women, not really sure why. One of the oldest parishioners came to me after the mass to congratulate me on such inspiring words. It felt great to hear that being new and all, but I must not let the praise get to me. I'm doing the Lord's work, and there's no place for vanity in it.

December 3rd, 2120,

Had a long conversation with Father Billingsley and Father Jones, today. I found out that both are strongly opinionated and that they believe the NAM is going to wreck this country apart. I don't know what to make of it just yet.

Yes, History speaks against them, but forgiveness is the most Christian thing to do. They won the elections fair and square, so they've earned the chance to rule according to their program. Voters will judge them come next election. Until then...

December 8th, 2120,

It has recently come to my attention that my Church, as beautiful as it is on the outside, is missing a few key things on the inside so I sent a detailed letter to the parish asking to see what they can do. I expect little, especially since it's Holiday Season, but no harm in trying.

(...)

December 21st, 2120,

Dear Father Mason,

Thank you for your letter. After reviewing your requests, the Parish has asked for additional funding to sort out the problems you mentioned. The first item on the list is the replacement of the church organ. The new one will be delivered shortly after the New Year. We will take care of all the other issues in due time. Merry Christmas!

Respectfully,

Cardinal Nathan Lane

(...)

"Hi, Mom. Voicemail again, seriously? I hate to be the bearer of bad news, but my flight just got canceled so I'm not making Christmas this year either. They're calling it 'the blizzard of the century' around here, and they're probably right. Please call me when you hear this so we can talk for real. Bye."

(...)

Excerpts from the journal of Father Theodore Mason

January 8th, 2121,

The church's new organ has arrived. I would have preferred the front row seats of the aisle taken care of first, but the church's priorities are what they are. The hymns sound beautiful when played on it though and everyone is excited so I guess I should be too?

January 23rd, 2121,

We've never had so many people in church until today. People are saying it's my presence that drives them, but one of my acolytes thinks differently. The young boy is head over heels over Ms. Harris, our organist, and it's easy to see why. Not only is she beautiful, she's also an expert player. Her mother is part of the NAM government and couldn't be prouder. Things are looking pretty good this year already. I'm glad.

January 29th, 2121,

Ms. Harris played something new today. I never heard anything like that. It was so exquisite and intoxicating... I almost drifted into a peaceful slumber listening to it. She says she'll be playing it for me every day from now on. I can't wait.

February 2nd, 2121,

Music... sweet music... how I love the way that organ sounds. Music...

(...)

February 12th, 2121,

Dear Father Mason,

There has been a change of plans. We will liberate no additional funds to St. Wellington's Church or any other church in the foreseeable future. Instead, you are to send us the entirety of your donations immediately to give to women. I take it you don't have any objections, but if that should be the case, please talk to Ms. Harris and listen to what she has to say. She'll know what you must do.

Respectfully,

Cardinal Nathan Lane, devoted servant of the Goddess.

(...)

Excerpts from the journal of Father Theodore Mason

February 13th, 2121,

I went to talk to Ms. Harris and found Father Billingsley and Father Jones kneeling at her feet. They were reciting a new rendition of Hail Mary that rings so true... I need to reproduce it. I have no choice.

"Hail Goddess, full of grace

Thy servants are with thee.

Blessed art thou in the world.

and blessed are the fruit of thy womb, women.

Holy Goddess, Mother of all,

Control us all, man slaves,

Now and at the hour of our death. Amen."

Music... sweet music... I too shall obey.

Writing Porn

Francis laid down the outline for his best friend's new short story on the kitchen island and muttered:

"Is this it?"

"Yes." Devon replied, holding a half-full bottle of beer in one hand and all his dreams and aspirations of being a talented writer in the other. "You don't like it?"

"Well, it's quite bland, and it doesn't scream 'best-seller' to me, that's for sure!"

"That's not a pleasant thing to say."

"Just telling it as it is. Even the synopsis at top sounds boring. What does a 'deconstruction of the post-postmodern woman' eve mean?"

"It's... you know what? Never mind. This was obviously a mistake." Devon snatched the white sheet of paper and stuffed it in the back pocket of his denim pants.

"Why are you so riled up?"

"Because I come to you asking for support and you immediately shut my ideas down, that's why? And it's not the first time either, Francis. You always do this."

"Don't shoot the messenger. You're a wonderful writer, but you focus on the wrong ideas, that's all. If you really want to be successful out there, try something different."

"Such as...?"

"Your chief character is disillusioned with the world men created, right? Have you thought about making her go lesbian then?"

"No, because that's not the point of your journey as I mentioned in paragraph four and..."

"Yeah, yeah." Francis interjected. "... but her journey is boring from start to finish and lesbians are hot. Also, that confidant she's supposed to meet along the way, the one with daddy issues? She could be a dominatrix and the two of them could have kinky sex. Tons and tons of kinky sex!"

Devon was appalled, face blank, eyes burning. "In other words, you want me to scratch my whole idea and write porn, instead!"

"And what's wrong with that? Porn sells! Go lesbian porn, mate! You won't regret it."

"Thank you so much for your perfectly worthless contributions. I have to go now."

"What? But I haven't even started on the hamburgers!"

"I just realized I'm no longer hungry. Now, if you'll excuse me, I have to get started on a boring journey."

Without another word, Devon stormed out, an angry man only a good dose of writing could soothe.

* * *

Three hours later, he sat twiddling his thumbs in front of a computer screen, all of his wonderful ideas reduced to frustrating gibberish. Ever since he had looked at writing as more than a hobby, he had published two short stories' collections, none of which had gained any traction. The lack of positive feedback hurt him more than he liked to admit. His family was completely indifferent to his fantasy escapades and now his closest friend wanted him to waste time with porn! It was madness.

Not that he had anything against porn. Just like everyone else, he often consumed it on lonely weekends, sometimes with lube, but most of them without. Porn was a wonderful stress reliever, but not something he called 'art'. He would never be caught writing something like...

Devon blinked when he noticed a particular sentence in the middle of the nonsensical constructions he had produced. It read:

"Ava slowly undid her satin dress to reveal a pair of mesmerizing supple breasts begging for a chance to penetrate the young teacher's mind."

That was something. Not perfect by any means, and yet there was a world of possibilities in it. Ava, the hypnodomme with a shady past. Jennifer, the blonde educator who was tired of dealing with men's tantrums, especially her co-workers. The story of how the two of them met on a rainy Sunday afternoon and began having fun exploring the depths of the human mind, grinding their pussies against one another and...

"Fuck it!" He reached for an energy drink from the mini-cooler next to his desk and got to work, producing lewd description after lewd description just for fun. He wrote one thousand words, then two thousand, ten minutes became twenty, one hour, two. The sun went down, and he was still typing, fingers almost fused to the keyboard as he described Ava in detail.

Shoulder-length jet-black hair with a single emerald highlight running along the right side of her face, aquamarine eyes, plump lips that could easily devour a man's cock if she were in the mood for it, hourglass figure made even more attractive by her PVC fetish. She was a sucker for shiny boots, leather collars, and improper uses of kitchen utensils. Hypnotizing people with a fork was one of her favorite pastimes.

The connections kept pouring in, liquid fever as dangerous as addictive. This could work. It had to! Time continued to flow mindlessly as he forgot the need to eat, go to the bathroom or sleep. At 5 am of the next day, he was still going.

And then, like a meteor had suddenly crashed on his head, he stopped, blinked again, and exclaimed:

"No way!"

* * *

Devon has been missing for over four months now. The police have no clue as to his whereabouts or what transpired prior to his untimely disappearance. The only witness account comes from a neighbor of his, octogenarian Mrs. Gold who, despite her weary eyes and failing memory, had this to say to the officers investigating the case:

"A black-haired woman appeared out of nowhere and dragged him out of the house on a leash! It was the weirdest thing I've ever seen."

About the author

S.B., Simple Being, middle name Creative. Writer and artist with a penchant for themes of Femdom Hypnosis and Mind Control. His thoughts are his own except when they're not.

Besides indulging himself in kinky delights, he loves his furry family of two (dogs), sci-fi and horror stories, and puns galore. He's also been writing a piece of erotic micro-fiction every single day since January 1st, 2016 and has no intention of stopping anytime soon.

Find out more and keep up with his latest extravaganzas by visiting and supporting his personal website, Spell... B-O-U-N-D.

9 798859 366343 6